# Twelve Stories from New Orleans

# TWELVE STORIES

## FROM NEW ORLEANS

MERLE HARTON

De Signis Press
*Ormond Beach*

The story "The Monger" was first published in *Back Porch Magazine* (Summer 1995).

Library of Congress Control Number: 2009906098

ISBN: 978-0-9824302-0-0

Published by De Signis Press
Ormond Beach, Florida USA

# Contents

---

# Finbar's Rebirth

On his 50th birthday, shy Finbar was visited by an angel who said that he could go through his life all over again, if he wanted to. He wouldn't be able to remember that he was going through life again, but he would have those occasional déjà vu episodes and just enough to enable him to make alternative choices. When he reached his 50th birthday again, the angel would return, he said, and Finbar would get this chance once more.

Finbar thought this over, prayed about it, and then decided that it was worth a try. So he kissed his childless wife good-bye, threw an enormous bundle of unpaid bills into the trash, slammed the front door of his unkempt, neglected home in rural

Louisiana, kicked the bald tires on his 15-year-old pickup truck, and told the angel, "Let's do it."

So Finbar went through life again. He emerged from his mother's womb again. He toddled around the same living room as before. He went to the same elementary school as he had the first time through. When he got to junior high, though, he had one of those déjà vu episodes, as the angel said he would. He was on his way to the lunchroom when that strange feeling of familiarity came over him and it delayed him enough so that he entered the lunchroom 12 seconds later than he had the first time in his life. That was enough of a delay to keep him from bumping into Scott DeMario, thus making it unnecessary for Scott to punch Finbar in the nose, which would mark Scott as a hard case and lead to eventual criminal behavior and later a long prison term, and which so humiliated Finbar that he became diffident and shy and ended up as a button salesman with a childless wife, many unpaid bills, an unkempt, neglected home in rural Louisiana, and a 15-year-old pickup truck with bald tires. That 12-second delay meant that Scott would actually grow up to be a well-appreciated state senator. It also meant that Finbar would make it through junior high school without losing confidence in himself, thereby enabling him, at the age of 19, to write a first novel (about angels, of all things) which crawled its way to the top tier of the New York Times bestseller list. This opened up opportunities for more celebrated novels, some well-received fiction collections, a Pulitzer Prize, and a happy marriage to a former Miss Florida, who bore him six children. He lived happily in his 8-bedroom home on the southern coast of Maine. His bills were all paid, and he got around in any of four late-model imported automobiles.

Life is good, he said as he reached his 50th birthday, the very same day confident Finbar was visited by the angel who said that he could go through his life all over again, if he wanted to.

The visit by the angel reawakened all of his memories, from the first time through life to the second and all of the choices he made, or didn't make, as the case may be. As before, said the angel, he wouldn't be able to remember that he was going through life once again, but he would have more of those occasional déjà vu episodes and just enough to enable him to make alternative choices. Also, as before, when he reached his 50th birthday again, the angel would return, he said, and Finbar would have this chance once more.

Finbar thought this over, prayed about it, and then decided that it was worth a try. So he kissed his beautiful wife good-bye, hugged each of his six children, took one last look at his checking account and investments, fondled his four late-model cars one final time, and told the angel, "Let's do it."

So Finbar again went through the same life. He emerged a third time from his mother's womb, and toddled around the same living room as before. He went to the same elementary school as he had both the first and second times through. When he got to junior high, though, he had another one of those déjà vu episodes, as the angel said he might. This time he was on his way to the library when that strange feeling of familiarity came over him and it delayed him enough so that he entered the school library 12 seconds later than he had the first time in his life. This brief delay was enough to keep him from reading L. Frank Baum's *Wizard of Oz*, which would have inspired him toward the literary career that had given him such fame and fortune in his second try at life. At least he was not punched in the nose by Scott DeMario again. Instead, it would be six years before he would happen to read Bertrand Russell's collection of essays on *Logic and Knowledge*, which inspired Finbar to study mathematical logic and which would lead him to philosophy, empiricism, logical positivism, atheism, and then a simple form of humanism.

Since being smart and good does not at all guarantee a successful life, let alone a happy one, this time Finbar reached his 50th birthday as a 9th-grade math teacher in the local public school; he had a plain wife, three children and a pit bull terrier, some unpaid bills, a small wood-frame home in rural Mississippi, and a classic Saab 900 with faded paint and two bad window motors.

On his 50th birthday, then, Finbar was visited by the angel who said that he could go through his life all over again, if he wanted to. Before the angel could utter another word, Finbar boldly announced that he did not believe in angels—he believed only in what could be verified through empiricism aided by mathematical logic. "Life is what it is," he said. He thanked the angel for the visit and then left him, like a *Watchtower* witness, on the front porch. The angel left, taking with him the reawakening of Finbar's memories, from the first time through life to the second and third, and all of the choices he made, or didn't make, as the case may be. ■

# Death Hurts Most the First Time Around

---

It was hot and the lawn mower I pushed seemed to move slower, slower … slower in fact than I was moving. I wondered whether this mower was as susceptible to the heat as I was. After all, it was a mere mechanical device. But then so was I—sort of. So I asked myself: was this push reel lawn mower actually slowing down by itself, as an act of free will, or was it just getting tired in the heat, slowing me down, forcing me to work harder? The end result would have to be that the two of us would just stop working. That seemed like a good idea to me.

I parked the mower in the shade of the single oak tree in the front yard and headed for the front porch and the tumbler of ice water. The ice was almost melted, but the water was still cold. I drank slowly and began to think of the utter stupidity of mowing a lawn. I looked around the corner of the porch at the mower standing against the oak tree. It seemed refreshed, in fact more refreshed than I was. I wandered back out into the yard. After all, I have an indomitable spirit and I would vanquish this yard. I turned and looked at our new house, our house of six months. It still looked impressive. Then, renewed with my indomitable spirit, I turned again to the yard.

There was not really much more to mow and the centipede grass in the yard offered little resistance to the whirling blades of the reel mower in front of me. A neighbor drove by and waved. I waved back, suspecting that as soon as he was out of sight he would start snickering at me and my classic reel lawn mower. There are not many of them in use today. Someone called it an old man's mower, which I took to be an intimation that what I was using was actually a piece of antiquity, an item of technology that had been supplanted by something vastly superior, something that was no longer made by hammer and anvil and a strong man standing over hot coals, but some part of a larger system which effected things bit by bit and then painted them and moved them into showrooms. I've used my share of power mowers. They're noisy, prone to frequent breakdowns, and I just hated having to get gasoline for the things. Besides, unless you use one of those mowers that can pull itself across the lawn, you still have to use your own energy to move a power mower over the grass, and they're in fact considerably heavier than the mower I was now pushing. Besides, my reel mower was cutting grass like precision scissors. The only thing it couldn't cut effectively was weeds.

There's something thoroughly sinister about weeds. Some of them are low-slung and spread out; cutting them only trims their tops, leaving them to sprawl outward. Others are tall, springing upwards, past the tops of the grass they intend to overcome, until they are valiant against my mower's blades, which was able only to push the tall weeds down until they could spring back up, almost triumphant, while the grass around it received its weekly clipping.

Weeds have an advantage over all other living plants. They have been almost entirely left alone to develop, against all the odds humans can throw at them. Poison strengthens them. Uprooting them only amuses them into moving about. Trimming them, cutting them to the same height and size as the grass around them, only gives them a guise which pleases them. They have a resilience and energy to survive what no other vegetable can endure.

I've heard about people who eat weeds. I have no problem with that. They can come over and eat my weeds any time. As a point of fact, there once was a famous man who ate all kinds of exotic plants and encouraged others to do the same. Not only did he eat weeds, but he ate things in lawns that you and I never even knew were there. He wrote books about it, and even ate tree bark. He died of stomach cancer. Now I don't know whether his cancer had anything to do with what he ate, but I do believe that moderation is a useful rule, if only because we have ample experience with the burdens of excess. Ask any alcoholic. And the Buddha recommended it, as did Confucius, although the latter did seem to spend an immoderate amount of time wandering around mainland China. Jesus didn't have much to say about moderation as a lifestyle choice, but I think he'd agree that if you're going to eat weeds, or tree bark, you should at least do so with some plan toward balancing your diet to include other foodstuffs we know to be healthful. Surely cancer is another way for the natural body to tell us that something is bad for us on the whole, or for some individual. Even this can promote a lesson of nature: eating weeds is bad for some people. Like sugar for the diabetic, salt for the hypertensive, animal dander for the asthmatic. In moderation, these things are not harmful. In abundance, they kill. Take exhaust from the modern combustion engine. It is bad enough to live in a country that cannot do without the combustion engine, but do I really have to cut my lawn with it?

Of course, I have seen (and used) some power mowers whose whirling blades have also had trouble with tall weeds, as though the weeds themselves had some kind of special coating that resisted sharp objects coming at them from the side. What are trees, anyway, but prehistoric weeds? These things in my yard would surely find a way to outlive any kind of lawn mower—or die trying. Such is that entity we call Nature.

But Nature isn't as generous with humans. It's not so much that we can't reason our way through a patch of weeds; it's rather that we get a plethora of choices in life and some of those just happen to be aesthetic. Surely it's the sense of aesthetics that prevents us from coexisting happily with weeds. How much simpler life would be without that curious sensibility.

Lacking a sense of aesthetics, we could buy food based on nutrient qualities alone, and not on smell or taste or packaging. We could all get around on public transportation, and there would be no graffiti to see; and if there were, we wouldn't care. We could get more things done, since television would not be a medium of entertainment but rather of information alone. Sex would be so much more accessible, if quantity over quality could coherently replace what is lost by the rituals of courtship and foreplay. Important people—that is, persons in political and ruling positions—would be required to keep diaries, for all histories would end up as chronologies. Music would no longer be a form of entertainment, but a tool of ceremony and of therapy. Our clothes would be simpler, and the choices would be solely utilitarian and economic.

How boring! But that was a comment from a man in an aesthetic mood. I've contradicted myself, you say? Okay, so I've contradicted myself. You figure out something better to do with these weeds bending down, as if it's all a great game, beneath the churning blades of my reel mower.

I'll be honest with you. I rarely attempt this in the blazing sun and the usual July heat in Louisiana, but today was different. I had a need to expend energy, which came out of nowhere this morning as I awoke to the realization that my friend Robert Joulissaint was dead. Forty-two was too young to die. If he had been an invalid or had succumbed to some exotic terminal illness or perhaps some rare congenital affliction which could have prepared me for his end—that, I think, would have made his death a transitional passage, something anticipatory, like the end of a movie. We know it's going to happen—and we accept it, like a fact.

Robert's death was more like you're watching a movie and the power goes out. Suddenness is really what makes Death a dangerous presence, because it's hardly ever predictable, and God knows we humans like predictability. That's why science eventually became so popular, once scientists figured out how to get it to work. In many ways, living without science is like living as a foreigner in a strange land. You never know when someone's going to walk up to you and say something you can't understand. It's really unnerving, having to live with that kind of unpredictability. Modern science now gives us a kind of translation, or perhaps a transliteration, of the language spoken by the natural world. It doesn't always say happy things, but at least now we anticipate the voice and fathom some of the grammar.

The yard was just about done. The grass clippings, aftermath of my precision lawn mowing, were strewn around like little cellulose hairs full of mineral water, ready to return their small treasures to the soil. Grass thrives on its own mulch. It is not cannibalistic, but with the aid of microbes what has been sloughed off becomes a kind of food. Strange, indeed, but then grass has its own natural agenda and the aesthetics of food never stands in its way.

Having mowed the lawn, my last task was to go around whacking down the weeds. The tallest ones I cut close to the ground with the whirling nylon strand from my rechargeable-battery-powered hand-held weed cutter. The most menacing of the weeds (especially those that looked as if they were bred to last longer than trees) I pulled up by hand. I would grab the unruly weed as close to the ground as possible, taking into my hand as much of the base as could be grasped, and pull upward. Sometimes I would get the entire rascal, roots and all. More often, though, I could only get the whole of the top, leaving the roots beneath the soil to taunt me at a later date with a new growth.

My pulling and tugging yielded some excellent devastation, as I omnipotently took it upon myself to expel from the universe as we know it future specimens of well-fitted survivalist weeds. One particular tough guy fought back, though, holding his ground with roots I imagined to extend three or four feet deep into the soil. I pulled until my back throbbed. I rose and rested and then quickly, as if to take him by surprise, grabbed a hold again and pulled. Almost all of it came out of the ground. A sliver of blade remained with roots attached. It was this piece of left weed that sliced through my index finger, right at the joint under my knuckle. Blood hurried from the wound. I wrapped it with the sweat band I kept around my head. That can't be the best thing for the wound, I thought, but then I had nothing else to use, other than my shirt or pants, both of which were as far from antiseptic as the band that was now turning red from the flow.

I watched my sweatband grow redder. If I were a 2nd-century Roman centurion, I'd be very concerned about the blood leaving my body; however, being a 21st-century suburban lawn warrior, I am less concerned about what is leaving my body than what may be going into this wound. It seems the more we know, the more we have to fear, especially of things that not even electron microscopes can disclose, things which exist only within the confines of a scientific theory. I thank God for my natural defenses, battalions of them, ready to battle the little microbes that waited on the weed's skin to enter a human fort and attack it from within. I was thankful for the helping hands of humans who found these things in theories and could conjure up, from their cerebral alembics, antidotes and cures to help my natural defenses, like reinforcements, cope with the new techniques of hitherto unknown intruders.

I pondered these wonders further as I went inside to wash my wound and apply a dressing. After all, I have an indomitable spirit and a little blood-letting wasn't going to buckle me.

"What happened?" Christine asked, catching me in the kitchen over the sink with my slashed hand under running water.

"I lost a battle but won the war," I answered.

"Oh."

"Is that all you can say? I am standing here, my life blood flowing into the sewer system, and all you can say is 'Oh'?"

Christine pulled some supplies from the cabinet above the toaster and came toward me. She was, as I then pictured her, a nurse with dressing for a soldier in a MASH unit. Her auburn hair, with a loud suggestion of red when the light shimmered just right, fell down in front of her face, a little curl dangling over her left brow.

"This ought to help," she said. I dried my hand and watched as she laid a quarter inch of antibiotic ointment on the cut and covered it with a Band-Aid. She straightened and looked at me with moist azure eyes. She smiled and a wrinkle appeared at the top of her nose. Her nose. She hated her nose. Too big, she said, but to me it was a perfect nose, or at least perfect for her face, which is the way noses are supposed to be on a pretty face.

"Thanks," I said, stealing a kiss.

"My hero," she said.

"Thanks again."

She searched my face. "You've had too much sun. Why don't you drink some water—not cold water, now—and then lie down and rest. You can shower later. Robert's wake is not until five."

"Will you wake me up?" I asked, taking a glass from the overhead cabinet.

"Yes, I'll wake you up."

I filled my glass with tap water, and drank it slowly before heading for the bed. I stretched out on my back and tucked under my head one of the small sofa pillows Christine had laid over the bed pillows. With my feet, shoes and all, dangling off the foot of the bed, I laid my arms up above my head and closed my eyes and—

"—Get up! Marc, wake up!"

I think there should be a study done on the sleep habits of men and women and on the differences that such a study would reveal. I really think more men are killed in their sleep than women.

This is so, I think, because men approach sleep with a double purpose: one, to sleep as soundly as is possible and, two, to sleep as often as possible. It's not that we would seek sleep were some other task set before us, but rather that the want of sleep overcomes us more often than it does women. I've heard reports of men who survive on five and six hours of sleep a day, but then I've been lied to before. Surely such men must die young. A man who sleeps well and sleeps often will live longer. He'll miss a lot of life, but what he does get out of life is more appreciated, since there is nothing like stepping out into the world after a really good rest. The key to the good rest, though, is to do so until your body wakes you; waking up before that natural alarm is like being half-sober.

"Marc! We have a wake to attend! Get up!"

So I got up, half-sober, but harboring the realization that women will never understand the importance of sleep for a man's total well-being. I hopped in the shower, dressed, and in a few minutes was presentable in my best dress clothes.

We left the house to our 13-year-old, Kimberly, and Marshall, who is 10, and drove out to the Hall of Eternal Peace mortuary, arriving at about 4:50. The parking lot was scattered with cars and we could see strangers walking in pairs into the mortuary. We parked and went up.

Inside was a young man dressed in black, as I was, except that my tie was louder than his. A message board directed us to the visitation for Robert Joulissaint.

The room was crowded with strangers, all with sad faces. I was sad, but not broken up. I was sad, but sad for these people. Death is something I've had to deal with before. Death to me is my father in a box, lying inanimate and as inaccessible to me as he was when he was a stranger. Death is my grandmother when I came home from 8th grade. Her broken hip kept her bedridden and helpless and I still get a weird feeling when I think about emptying her bedpan. It was not the bedpan but the look on her face that haunts me. When I came home that day, my father came to the door and said, "Your grandmother just died," and he looked sad, but he was only wearing the mask of a sad person; behind that mask was a man whose emotions were as hollow as his words to me. My mother was in tears; this was real sadness and I knew that. As I walk into my grandmother's bedroom, which she shared with my two sisters, there was an unsettling calm. Before me on the bed, lying still was a dead body, yet a peaceful piece of amber. Before she died, she told my mother, who was not expecting her death, "Papa is coming for me." This saddened my mother, because she believed her. My grandmother possessed a sensitivity that my mother, too, was given. She read the Taro cards and could, even without the cards, amaze her listeners with her prophetic words. My mother believed her, and so did I. My grandmother's foreknowledge of her own death brought her not terror but relief and joy.

Birth and death are sort of opposites, but it's a shame that we don't deal with them in the same way. I mean, at least we can anticipate a person's birth: we know what is about to transpire and prepare for it and celebrate it. There was once an obese woman who went into Charity Hospital complaining of a stomachache. The pain subsided when she gave birth to a baby boy. Only in the rarest of cases do we find birth by total surprise. On the other hand, death almost always surprises us. If only we could prepare for it, as my grandmother was partly able to do, and to celebrate it, as another real part of being human.

But then I'm not in control of my society. I don't make the rules. I can comment on them and make recommendations, but alone I can do nothing. I could, I suppose, run right on over to Robert's body, turn to the crowd of mourners, and with a smile rejoice: *He's dead! That's great! He was a miserable man—you all know that! Hey, now, why the long faces? Come, let us celebrate his newly found peace! Grab your hymnals! Let us sing! What? Selection twenty-three, "Is My Team Ploughing?" Excellent choice! All together now....*

"Marc. Are you all right?" That was Christine. She had her hand on my arm and she was moving me through this crowd of sad faces. We made our way among a swarm of bodies, until I was face to face with a woman who was sobbing uninhibitedly. As she cried, she kept her eyes closed, but I think she had no choice: her eyes were closed shut by a potent grief, the kind of grief that makes you want to shut out entirely this world of light, this world of smiles and flesh pressed gently and blushed cheeks and a bright sun-lit bedroom on a late Saturday morning and sun showers on a garden of pretty many-colored flowers which wait in patience for the tender hand of a lover who will exchange them.

"Ellen, we're so sorry about Robert." That was Christine again, speaking to the sobbing wife of my dead friend. Ellen was surrounded by others who were encouraging this party of sadness. Really, who would want to attend this kind of party? There was no music, no noisemakers, just silence and moans; no dancing allowed, only standing, now on one foot and now on another, and sitting with hands clasped and talking with voices that you would only use on an occasion such as this; no balloons, only flowers—lots of flowers—in extravagant displays around the room, on tri-part stilts, in big jars that no kid would ever think of picking cookies out of, in ugly tall green glass vases with scarab-like bumps all over, in arrangements that Nature alone had never conceived and placed there by hands especially skilled in the killing of lovely vegetation. But forget about the many colors: there were a thousand fragrances wherever you pointed your nose; there was rose, tulip, chamomile, magnolia, jasmine, and new light sweet odors that could be flowers, but perhaps not; there were smells that evoked images of sea and wind, and of leather, and of wood; there were thick heavy maple fragrances and sharp pine and exotic spices and strange mixed concoctions, like those that cling to your clothes after passing by the department-store beauty counter, and rouge and fruit-flavored lip-sticks, and astringent lotions, and five kinds of bath oils, and animal musk, and smells that may hide luring pig pheromones; and there were a hundred soaps—deodorant soaps, detergent bars, skin-softening cold cream-filled beauty soaps, soaps in funny shapes that sit in a small pile near the sink in the guest bathroom.

And nowhere was there a hint of dead flesh. And the woman cried, because in this room was a mass of dead flesh, but it was flesh that had been made up to look as if it were alive but asleep, animated but now at rest, a living force that could not now be quickened. And the woman cried because she knew no better than anyone else around here how again to touch something that had once been warm and vital, or how to speak to someone who was no longer there. Robert Joulissaint was dead and she could not deal with that. And she cried openly because her grief could not be contained in the gaping wound in her chest. And she could not stop crying because God would not comfort her and the mortals she was left with were blind apprentices, unskilled and possibly with little potential for the mastery over emotions that death asks us to challenge.

And I spoke to this woman, the wife of my friend, but with words I do not now recall. And she spoke out loud, perhaps to me, perhaps to the group around her, about the health of her husband, the suddenness of his death, and the events that preceded it. And as she spoke, still I heard nothing.

And I left the woman weeping and walked to the casket to pay my last respects to my friend who was waked. How peaceful he was. The tanned face and the tanned hands crossed on his chest were unfamiliar to me. Robert was always pale, for he was always inside some building or other, whether at work or at home, and sheltered in transportation by a car. And I thought of the last time I had been with my friend, as we sat together during some dinner occasion at his house and talked about computers, his in particular, and the programs he used and desired and the best ways to optimize the equipment he had.... And I looked long at his face, trying to picture him upright, since I had never seen him lying down, and trying to see him as the pale man I knew before, beneath the makeup, for I knew that his natural color must now be yellow-brown, the color of amber, like my grandmother Andersen. And I accepted that he was not sleeping: he was dead.

This was death, where someone we love is no longer responsive to our words and the flesh is still, and amid the tumult of emotions and memories there is a fleeting feeling of peace and compassion and a happiness in the small thought that this being cannot feel, like a living human, the pain we feel at the suddenness of a departure toward a place we do not know. This was death, this being now changed; an inanimate thing, yet somehow still a person, which held within it something unspoken, something that could be discharged if I touched it, or even neared it, like a hot spark.

And Christine and I left the wake, saying our goodbyes as we walked out. And we got in the car to leave. And I frightened Christine then, because she had never seen me cry. And I was frightened, too, because I could not control the tears, and I did not remember how to stop this and I sobbed in a voice I did not recognize. And with my hands on my face I tried to cover my eyes and my mouth, but still I continued to cry, and I cried until the memories hurt me no longer. ■

# Funerals

Funerals in New Orleans can really be fun, but only if you happen to be important enough to deserve a Jazz Funeral. In a Jazz Funeral all the participants get to follow the corpse to the cemetery while dancing to cool jazz sounds in a kind of small Mardi Gras parade. Really, there's nothing like the rhythmic blast of a brass horn to get you back into the appreciation of life. The only prerequisite for a Jazz Funeral is that you have to be black. For us white folks, well, our funerals are as dull as all the rest. You know, sadness, weeping, dressed in Sunday best, nodding off during the ceremonies, etc.

When my Uncle Henry died, I foreknew it would be another dull wake and another dull funeral ceremony. I was kind of hoping Grandpa John would be at this funeral. He hated dull, and always managed, one way or another, to liven things up a bit. Perhaps that's why he was somehow kept away from our family funerals. Besides, he was well into his eighties and locked in, safely out of the way, at a rest home.

So there we were, the whole family and a lot of strangers and me and my live-in girlfriend, Christine, sitting in rows of pews in a dull quiet church with the dead body of my Uncle Henry reclining in the front. The ceremony was just about to begin, though, when in walked Grandpa John. He wasn't exactly walking; it was more like he was shuffling and sliding his way down the aisle, with a little help from a foxy blonde attendant from the rest home. As the low shouts of "What is he doing here?" and "Who let him out?" turned into less audible grumbles and mutters, Grandpa John and the blonde settled into a pew in the second row from the front. The funeral ceremony began.

It was dull from the beginning. The priest did his ritual things and there was praying and bowing of heads and kneeling, up and down, up and down, and a hundred long readings from the Bible.

The only one who remained stationary during all of this was Grandpa John. That is, until halfway through the ceremony, when he slowly started leaning over to the left. His blonde attendant pushed him back up. Then he leaned to the right. His blonde attendant pulled him back over. He kept doing this, until he finally got to lean way over to the right; suddenly, loudly, he cleared his throat. The blonde attendant grabbed him again and pulled him back upright. There were titters and snickers from the kids around him, but they were hushed up by adults who as quickly shot daggers of disapproval at Grandpa John. A moment later, he leaned over to the left and loudly cleared his throat again. A few more snickers and a couple of laughs, this time from some adults. The blonde pushed him over and then appeared to scold him in hushed tones. Some of the people around my Grandpa John were getting annoyed, and as he continued to lean over and clear his throat, they started moving away from him, shaking their heads in disgust. Toward the end of the ceremony, the second pew from the front was empty except for Grandpa John and the blonde.

At the conclusion of the festivities, I woke up Christine, who had been snoozing on my shoulder and was just beginning to snore, and everybody started filing out. On the way to the exit door, I heard a couple of my cousins complain about Grandpa John. "So what's the fuss?" I asked them as we made our way through the aisles. "He's an old guy and he was just clearing his throat." Responded my cousins in unison: "Sure, he was clearing his throat." I think that was sarcasm. They left in a huff, refusing even to attend Uncle Henry's burial.

A couple days later, I decided to go to the Lakeside Rest Home to visit Grandpa John. When I got there, he was sitting quietly on a porch swing with the blonde attendant. I went up and introduced myself and sat down in a wooden chair beside him, close enough so that at the right moment I could look up the blonde's skirt. We chatted about the weather and then about nothing in particular.

After a moment, Grandpa John started leaning over to the side. The blonde attendant pushed him upright. Then he leaned over to the other side, and the blonde pulled him back up. This went on until the blonde, now looking weary, said she had to go take care of someone else for a minute and asked me to watch Grandpa John. I said okay.

After she was gone, I asked him, "What was that all about?"

"Well," he said. "Sometimes a man has to toot his own horn." With that, he leaned way over to the side, looked straight at me and, giving me a wink, abruptly cleared his throat, at the same time releasing from the other end a raucous fart. ∎

# The Look

I have just completed a major sociological study whose results are so astounding as to invite immediate publication, my receipt of every important award for scientific excellence in the field of projective statistics, at least six months' worth of rounds on the television talk-show circuit, solicitations to lecture at each of the Ivy League colleges, and critical discussions in all international scientific journals. Famous photographers will surely bicker among themselves over who will be first to snap a black-and-white portrait of me in some candid pose, or at least with my hair mussed up. Journalists will camp out on my front lawn, hoping for a chance to jot down some quotable words from me. My friends will pass each other in the supermarket and comment on how they knew all along that I had it in me. Old men will drink beer in VFW halls and pass my name around the room like a chum, and the tabloids will make up fantastic stories about me (as told to them by a close friend, or a reliable source). Not only will I have the key to the city, but the White House guards will know me on a first-name basis. The phone calls will not stop and my mailbox will be full every day, and I may even have to hire a harem of secretaries and a dozen Xerox machines just to satisfy the demands from every *Who's Who* and encyclopedia publisher in need of a copy of my curriculum vitae. Indeed, my findings are that impressive, as they ensure my immortality. For on the subject of my study, using my own proprietary calculus to achieve these results, I have determined (with an insignificant margin of error) that regardless of the exact date you may wish to determine your outset, at the end of another fifty years nearly everyone will be more confused than they are now.

Having completed my statistical analysis of this timely phenomenon, I can with confidence also say, of the subject of my study, that if anything can be said to be worse than going through adolescence, it is the experience of it a second time. And every parent is condemned to have that second experience.

The horror of that experience came to me when my daughter Kimberly dropped head first into the pit of adolescence. Puberty was not a fun time for her, and she wanted to be sure that I knew it. To add to the pain of the experience, my new interest in a new business did nothing to help my extremely delicate relationship with Kimberly.

Our problems started, I think, when we made our move to the new house. I know this because of the look she gave me when Christine and I announced the move. Oh, it was not just the house. It was the timing of it all. At the time, she was 13; she had already started shaving her legs, she had already had her first period, boys were an interesting species to her, and she was finishing the eighth grade and planning on entering the local high school, with all of her friends, as a freshman. Moving to a new house, a new town, a new neighborhood, a new school—add to these the hormonal juices that were flowing freely inside of her, and you get a very unhappy teenager. It was THE LOOK that gave it away.

She had given me numerous immature versions of THE LOOK several times as she was growing up, but it was never so clearly maturely defined and punctuated as the time I took her—she was about 8 or 9 at the time—to a candy factory in New Orleans on a free tour of the facility. It was a factory that specialized in jellies that were "made with real fruit!" These jellies, called Elfkin Fruit Snacks, were in vogue for a good part of Kimberly's childhood; they were good for snacks and great for lunches carried to school, since they came wrapped about ten to a packet, and they won our parental approval because, unlike candy, these were "made with real fruit!" To her, though, they were just another snack, but she liked them and seemed to take comfort in the thought that we cared enough to include in her diet a snack that was "made with real fruit!"

So there we were in the factory. Our guide was someone from the marketing department who was on the company's speaker's bureau, which meant that he had to rotate with others in his department on giving these tours through the factory. It was something new his department head had conjured up, and the statistics that he placed in individual piles on their conference table and displayed graphically in pie, bar, and line charts all suggested a marketable increase in the sales of their products after such tours are given. I learned this when I commented on how nice it was that he had given up his Saturday to wear a suit and tie and lead total strangers around a noisy factory.

In any case, we were shown how five or six different candies were made, from their start as milk and sugar and special flavors to the chocolate coating and wrapping and their final run down a conveyor to boxes. And then with obvious pride our guide led us to another part of the factory, where the Elfkin Fruit Snacks were prepared.

The first part of this sub-tour started with the washing of various fruits they called the "pastel fruits," perhaps because of their color, or perhaps because of their commonness. These were oranges, grapes, lemons, strawberries, and cherries. They zipped by in groups on a conveyor and were washed with jets of water, and then disappeared into another room where, said our guide, they were peeled and sliced and "prepared for special processing into Elfkin Fruit Snacks." We got to spend a lot of time watching the fruit go around and around in the washer and then disappear into another room. From there we were taken to a room where several aromatic liquids were boiling in large brass vats. This, said our tour guide, was the final processing of the Elfkin Fruit Snacks before being poured into molds and then cooled and placed in wrappers.

As we stood watching the cauldrons boil, smelling the great smells of oranges, grapes, lemons, strawberries, and cherries, a man walked slowly over to one of the cauldrons. This was the quality-control taster, said our guide. He must have weighed over 350 pounds and his stomach tested the durability of the buttons of his white lab coat. He had an enormous round face, with a few sprigs of hair on the top, and a fat flabby lower lip that dribbled saliva. He came right up to the vat and pulled from the side a large ladle and then he waved aside some of the steam and dipped the ladle into the liquid. He pulled the ladle up, blew on it a few times and then took a sip. He rolled his eyes around in large exaggerated circles and then swished the liquid in his mouth a few times. Suddenly his eyes bulged. He spat the liquid back into the vat and shouted, "So you think I got everything in here? Who's the joker? Where's the fruit? Well, where's the fruit? Get Joe in here!"

The fat man stood there until Joe came in. Joe was a thin black man, somewhere in his twenties, who carried with him a small plastic bag full of a powder resembling flour. The big man said some angry things to Joe, raising his short arms up and down like a baby bird on a first flight, and then screamed, "This can't go out like this! You forgot the fruit!" He then grabbed Joe and put him in a headlock, his stubby arms barely making the circumference about the man's head. He pulled him over to the vat, but at such an angle from where we stood that all we could see was a mass of white with a black anguished head emerging from the bulk. "When you get to be a taster," the fat man shouted, "you'll come to appreciate what real fruit can do to the taste of this broth! If you ever get to be a taster! And you can bet your black ass that you won't make this mistake again!" He let Joe loose and the black man jumped back. "Now, where's the measured quantity of fruit that should be in this vat?" At that, Joe, moving quickly, reached into his pocket and pulled out a teaspoon and threw in 3 small scoops of the white powder from the plastic bag. The fat man responded with a look of contempt and reached for another object, a long wooden stick, and with that he stirred the boiling liquid a couple of times and then started drooling again and stuck the ladle in and tasted the concoction once more. He rolled his eyes as he had done before, and then swallowed loudly and shouted: "Ah! The fruit! Now that's the stuff of Elfkin Fruit Snacks!"

We all stood stiff with mortification. At this point the guide collapsed on the floor. We shuffled around and tried to revive him with slaps to his cheeks, some of us using more vigor than others, until he finally got up. With a face the color of chalk, but still to our relief, he announced the end of the tour. I looked over at Kimberly. She was standing to the side, staring at me—giving me THE LOOK.

Not only did she give me THE LOOK when we announced the move, but she gave me THE LOOK again when I announced that she would be matriculating in her first year in high school in a reputable Catholic school for girls, the exclusive (and expensive) St. Jeanne D'Arc Academy. The tuition was high, and we had to squeeze some items from our budget in order to accommodate the expense, but she was worth it. She did not like it, however, no matter what the expense.

The school was, at least in my opinion, the best opportunity for a young woman. It was sexually segregated, giving her fewer distractions than if she were in a co-ed school; she had to wear a uniform, thus reducing those tensions that fashion forces upon the peer-impressionable young; the school was all college preparatory, encouraging a scholastic excellence and interest in learning that could only aid Kimberly in a competitive world; the school had a strong female teaching force, which gave her a large pool of possible role models.

The principal, Mrs. Olivette Skiverson, seemed the perfect model of what the school could do: She was not unattractive, with bright green eyes and a complexion so clear and smooth as not to require make-up, perhaps a clean result of chastity or formative years spent in a nunnery. She wore dark-frame glasses to suggest a scholarly inclination, and shoulder-length natural brown hair with a natural curl, suggesting modesty, a decent upbringing, and an unpretentious lifestyle. A perpetual but warm smile added genuineness to her manner, which was always friendly; and joined to this was an administrative talent, which she had to have to keep such a school in the top ranks of girls' academies for five years straight. Mrs. Skiverson was a woman so well-planned as to be almost molded for perfection.

And then there was Ms. Weils, the assistant principal, a woman of charm, intelligence, and physical beauty—surely this was a role model if ever there was one. After a moment's meeting with Mrs. Skiverson, the three of us—two wall-eyed parents with one young woman in tow—went to the small office of Ms. Weils, who proceeded to interview Kimberly on why she wanted to attend St. Jeanne D'Arc Academy.

*Because she gets to wear a uniform and she would not be under pressure to dress in the latest fashions, and because the school will prepare her for college.*

Kimberly sounded like someone who had been coached, like a beauty contestant answering one of those intellect-testing questions before a panel of judges. What were her hobbies? She had no hobbies, it seemed, but she liked to read, and had started (but never finished) *Gone with the Wind.* That was good, said Ms. Weils, because they encourage reading at St. Jeanne D'Arc Academy. Here, for that matter, was a reading list for the year. Ms. Weils produced a scroll on which was etched every classic ever written since the dawn of western civilization, some of which I did not even recognize, but then I had to look fast as the scroll slipped from Ms. Weils' grasp and unrolled, sending a twenty foot sheet to the floor, out the door, and down the hall. As I offered to gather the document together, Ms. Weils took Kimberly's school records, which were part of the registration packet, and questioned Kimberly on her favorite subjects. English was on top and then Algebra, which came out of the blue. Ms. Weils instructed us to follow the hall down to the registrar's office, where her courses would be scheduled and final paperwork would be completed. We thanked Ms. Weils, and with the two-pound scroll under my arm I followed Christine and Kimberly out the door and down the hall.

The school was small, matriculating only 150 students each year, so it was not as though any girl could just walk up and register there. Once there, though, the competition was keen, but it was competition among peers, competition among young women eager to excel in studies and to challenge themselves and to strengthen those talents which would be needed in a modern arena that was not professionally encouraging to women. Over 98 percent of the graduates of St. Jeanne D'Arc went on to college, and 50 percent of those continued into graduate school: so said the pamphlet Christine and I studied as we planned our daughter's future, before I bravely, stalwartly, with my chest thrust forward like a Canadian Mountie, marched through the tangled thicket of future defeat and cut a swath with wide exaggerated thrusts of my machete—my pen, I mean, for I really was excited as I signed my name twice to the 8 1/2 by 14 inch three-part tuition loan form, not even considering the cost, for my daughter was worth any such exertion. And what did dear Kimberly think of the new school? I was thankful at the time that she did not give me THE LOOK. "Oh, we'll see," she said with a sly grin.

And see we did. Within the very first semester at St. Jeanne D'Arc Academy, Kimberly went from a straight-A student to a submariner, that is, someone delving deeply below C-level, and then deeper to the dark Ds, and then to the horrible depths of the Fs. As she sank, or swam along the bottom, as the case may be, it became clear that someone with her preparation was not working at full potential. In fact, she was not even trying. Really, if it were in my power to do it all over again, and to do so knowing what I know now, and if I could possibly do so with wide-alert, superhuman, knowledgeable but uncaring detachment—if I could alter things for my own thoroughly selfish satisfaction, I would then be in a position to offer to every new parent this advice: Before your children reach adolescence, seriously consider selling them to the highest bidder; or try to work out some sort of lease-purchase arrangement; or, at the very least, have them spayed.

Not only did she flunk nearly every course, the exceptions being Religion and Physical Education, but the school counselor, a Mrs. Hellman, sent us a nice letter notifying us that Kimberly was being placed on academic probation and that "as demanded by our Student Handbook, page 3, Kimberly will be required to attend after-school help sessions regularly as well as a mandatory study session two days each week." Did this bother Kimberly? Not in the least. She was trying hard, she said, but there was always a suggestion of insincerity in her voice whenever she responded in that way to our entreaties for her to study harder, do her homework, let us help her with her schoolwork, participate in class, read, read, read. Nothing fazed her. Two weeks after receiving Mrs. Hellman's letter, we made an appointment to talk with her.

On the appointed day, as we walked through the school to Mrs. Hellman's office, we had to pass through the school library, where I got to see about ten normal SJD students (in white blouses, plaid skirts, white socks, sensible shoes) reading or studying or researching, the usual serious school stuff, at several round tables set up in the library. There was no snickering, no throwing spitballs, no defacing school property—these were young women working their way into academic excellence, learning from the past so that they may make advances for the future of humankind, taking advantage of the resources of an excellent educational institution to better themselves and to lay up a store of knowledge that they can use in a satisfying, if not lucrative, profession. That, at least, was how it seemed to me as we made our way to Mrs. Hellman's office.

Mrs. Hellman greeted us at the door to her closet-sized office. Christine sat in a chair in the corner of the room and I sat near the door and the school counselor sat at her desk, which put her about a foot away from us. We broke the tension of the cozy arrangement with chit-chat. I commented to Mrs. Hellman that it was nice to see that people were still using the Apple II computer, since I could not escape the Apple IIe sitting behind her. She seemed not to think much of it, for she simply gave me a nod and then crossed her legs and responded to Christine's remark about how exciting a school counselor's job must be.

"It's hell," Mrs. Hellman said, swatting the air. "It's pure hell. It's bad enough having to help these girls with choices of universities, or local colleges, or—gag—some proprietary school, but having to lead them to make those choices, well, it's absolute hell. I tell you, you wouldn't want to be in my shoes."

I knew what she meant, but I looked at her shoes anyway. They were burgundy penny loafers, with shiny pennies in them. She caught me looking at the shoes and, with quick upright jerk of her back, planted her feet flat on the ground and put both hands on her knees and gave me the kind of look a woman gives when a man has been trying to look up her skirt.

"Well," she said officiously, "we're here to discuss Kimberly's progress, aren't we now?"

Both Christine and I nodded. Mrs. Hellman reached over and pulled a sheet of paper from a folder on her desk.

"Well," she said, waving the paper at us before holding it in front of her face, as if to study it. "I see that we have a challenge ahead of us. Kimberly needs to earn a C average in Spanish for the second semester if she is to receive full credit for the course for the year; she must earn a D average in Algebra I and English I for the second semester. I caution you that a failure in more than one subject would place Kimberly's future at SJD in jeopardy."

"What do you mean?" I asked, now breaking into a sweat.

"No student can fail more that one course and return to school the following year. A single failure will require that she attend summer school here; I know that the public school will permit two summer school courses, but we allow only one. There have been rare exceptions, where a student with more than one failure was allowed to return the next year, but this is a matter that is to be decided by Mrs. Skiverson, the principal, according to very specific criteria." At that she gave me an exaggerated wink. "Now, as for Spanish, I think that's just a lost cause. The year is half over, the coursework is cumulative, and I think Kimberly's time would be better spent in bringing up the other grades, leaving Spanish for summer school. Now, I've asked Kimberly to join us. Let's see what she thinks of all this and whether we can get a commitment from her on her future here."

Before we could say anything, before we could discuss the matter apart from our daughter's presence and intervention, Mrs. Hellman was on the phone to someone and barking to send Kimberly in. Before she could put the phone down, we heard a faint knock on the door and then it was opened and in walked Kimberly. She was dressed in her school uniform, a white blouse with plaid skirt, but on top of the blouse she wore a tattered red flannel shirt. Under the skirt she wore tight black stretch pants. On her feet, instead of the regulation saddle oxfords, she wore black-and-white canvas high-top sneakers, with something scribbled all over the white walls. Cupped in her left hand was a chunk of some huge pastry from which she tore large parcels with her right hand and stuffed them in her mouth as she walked. From my perspective, and how I felt at that moment, looking up from the floor, she might as well have been wearing nothing at all and chewing on a 5-pound smoked salmon. She was all smiles for Mrs. Hellman, but barely glanced in our direction, as she took the last chair in the tiny room to the right of the counselor and sat down and faced all three of us. She kept smiling and stuffing her face with the pastry, which seemed to keep its size no matter how much she pulled from it.

"Well, Kimberly, your parents and I have been talking about your progress here as SJD, and it seems we have some difficult choices to make now, while we still have a chance to do something about this."

Mrs. Hellman repeated the situation to our daughter just as she had said it to us, along with her suggestion for Kimberly's course direction.

"Now do you suppose you can bring these grades up, Kimberly? I know you have the ability to do it. Your standardized test scores certainly indicate your aptitude for them. Are you unhappy here?"

Kimberly stuck the last wad of pastry in her mouth and chewed. "I don't like it here," she announced, letting large crumbles of dough fly from her mouth. "I don't have any friends here. I want to go to the public high school—that's where all my friends go."

She continued, and I let her go on about the cruelty of her teachers and the coldness of the students at SJD, for I was back down on the floor again, looking up like a bug. Christine's face was the color of stone, and she bore a faint smile, the involuntary kind, like someone caught doing something wrong. Mrs. Hellman listened intently, but with the knowing look of someone who had heard this all before. Kimberly finished her peroration, at last, and then folded her arms, promised to try harder in her school work, and sat back in her chair with a smuggish simper on her face. I was back in my own chair again, but a weaker man than before.

"Well, thank you, Kimberly." Mrs. Hellman closed the folder and put in back on her desk. "That will be all. You may return to your classes now."

Kimberly got up and went to the door. She opened it and started to walk out; as she did, she turned with a brisk whip of her head and, staring straight at me, proceeded to give me THE LOOK. In a moment she was gone and the door was closed.

No sooner had the door shut than someone else walked in. She was blond, very thin, about 4 feet high, and obviously retarded.

"Momma," she said, coming into the room.

"Oh, hi, Kate." Mrs. Hellman hugged the child. "This is my daughter, Kate," she said to us by way of introduction. "Now, Kate, these are the Andersens and they're here to talk with me about their daughter. Now you go wait outside. We're just about finished."

Kate's pale cheeks were now flushed. She smiled at her mother and then at us and dutifully went back outside.

"My daughter is seventeen, but she has the mind of an eight-year-old, although in some ways she is very advanced and perceptive."

"She seems to have a very sweet personality," I said, expressing my first impressions.

"Oh, she's a real nice person. Well, thank you for coming. I will monitor Kimberly's progress, but I'd like you to reinforce what we do here at SJD by encouraging her in her studies, and especially in those after-school help sessions."

That elicited a harmony of nods from Christine and me, and we both agreed to do what we could to assist our daughter in improving her scholastic standing at the school. We thanked her and walked out. I left the door slightly ajar, since I expected the retarded child Kate to hurry inside. Instead, I found her right outside, standing very still, in the hallway.

"Your little girl is having problems, isn't she?" Kate said to me as I passed.

"Yes, she is, Kate." I stopped and looked down at the pale but happy face of Mrs. Hellman's daughter. "And I wish I knew what exactly is wrong."

"Oh, that's easy," she said, glowing with a smile. She bent her head forward and pointed several times to the back of her neck and then straightened up and hurried into her mother's office. Before closing the door behind her, she looked straight at me, gave me another smile, and announced: "It's called a hypothalamus!" ∎

# Dinner at Antoine's

It was sometime in April, and a doctor friend of mine and his wife were in town for a conference, and he gave me a call and wanted me and my live-in girlfriend Christine to go out to dinner with them. "Sure," I said. The dinner was free, after all. Since they wanted to go down to the French Quarter, I suggested Galatoire's, on Bourbon Street. It's a great place to eat and, besides, with all the mirrors and tiles around the wall, it looks just like a men's washroom and I thought that would really help to convey the spirit of New Orleans to my visitors. But instead they wanted to go to Antoine's, I guess because they liked wood floors and dim lights and big expensive bills. "No problem," I said. Anyway, the dinner was free.

So we all met down at Antoine's at eight o'clock and went inside. We were directed to a nice table upstairs and a waiter named Paul came by with his hand out and took our order. It was a big meal. We started with Oysters Rockefeller, Oysters Thermidor, and then fried oysters on toast buttered with paté de foie gras and smothered in the restaurant's Colbert sauce. Everybody else had something different to eat for the main course, but I ordered a plate of Oysters Bienville and the house salad. Obviously something was missing from my diet and I was having a craving. Besides it was an "R" month and that meant the oysters would be firm, not mushy.

About midway through the meal, though, the oysters began to have an effect on me. My doctor friend's wife, Rebecca, was just chatting away and then, as if by accident, her hand brushed against my knee. But then she did it again. Hey, that time it was no accident! And then Christine started rubbing her hand on my other knee and giving me winks and smiles. I imagined for a moment that I was James Bond in a kilt, being fondled during dinner at a ski resort. Rebecca started stroking my knee and giving me smiles and winks, too. Wait, this was really happening!

Then the waiter named Paul came by with his hand out and asked if everything was all right and proceeded to name all the desserts on a cart being wheeled around the room and waved a tall black man in a white busboy coat over to pour thick chicory coffee into our porcelain cups. I was at this point very light-headed and the room was starting to spin. The blood was going somewhere besides my head, but I couldn't be sure just where.

Then the maître de came by with an old-fashioned phone in his hand—the black kind with a big receiver and a rotary dial—and trailed a long cord behind him. He looked around the room and announced that there was a phone call for a Mr. Randolph Peirce. Christine and Rebecca just kept smiling and winking at me and stroking my knees, moving their hands up and down my thighs.

"Paging Mister Randolph Peirce," said the maître de. "Mister Randolph Peirce? Mister Randolph Peirce."

Suddenly I jumped up and threw my arms in the air and shouted: "Garçon! Here, Garçon! I'm Randy! I'm Randy! It's true! I'm Randy!" As I rose, though, I caught the corner of the table and tipped it over and everything slid off onto the lap of my doctor friend.

Afterwards, standing on Saint Louis Street, outside Antoine's, Rebecca said what a wonderful meal she had and, with a wink, thanked me for showing her such a fun time. My doctor friend was still inside the main entrance with our waiter named Paul. With one hand Paul was wiping down his front with a big napkin, all the while holding out his other hand, into which my doctor friend stuffed dollar bills. I could tell, even through the beveled glass doors, that my doctor friend was not pleased by the experience.

As for Christine, all she could say to me was: "Shame on you. That was the worst Scottish accent I've ever heard in my life." ∎

# The Drive By

My friend Hank was a man known for his committed Christian faith, a mature walk with God, and his equally sincere interest in simplicity. He was also renowned for his car, a real piece of junk. As a company president in metro New Orleans, it wasn't like he couldn't afford a new vehicle, but he kept it because he didn't want to appear ostentatious by driving a later-model car.

The one time I got to ride with Hank in his car was an adventure.

It was the day my car was in the shop. I got a ride to work but didn't know how I was going to get back home. When I got to my office, I took a moment and bowed my head for a quiet request that someone would be available to give me a lift home after work. Within half an instant—maybe less—the phone rang. It was Hank.

"I heard you needed a ride today," he said. "It's ninety-five miles out of the way, but I'd be happy and honored if you'd let me drive you home."

"How did you know I needed a ride?" I asked.

"Oh, gee," he said, "I thought everybody knew."

I decided not to touch that one. I said: "But, Hank, you know my house is only about TWELVE miles away. It's not NINETY-FIVE miles."

"Ah, it may *seem* like twelve miles," he said. "But if you're in the right frame of mind, it turns out to be almost exactly ninety-five miles."

I didn't get that one, either. We agreed to meet in front of the main building right after work.

So at the end of the workday I stood out in front of the main building and waited. I heard a distant clamor. The noise got louder. It was precisely the sound nine Coast Guard helicopters make just before they crash! I dove into the ditch and covered my head with my briefcase. The noise was thunderous now, unbearable, and it was coming right towards me. This was it. Armageddon. This was the big one. Then it stopped. I heard a car door open. And then footsteps. I peeked out from under the briefcase and saw Hank's shoes. I jumped up and brushed myself off, feeling totally humiliated.

"You know, every once in a while I like to lie down and push my face in a ditch, too," he said with a gentle smile. "It really gives you that close-to-nature feeling, don't you think? Come on now, we should get going."

I looked at his car. "Isn't that an antique?" I asked.

"Not yet," he said. "A couple more years to go."

We walked over to the car, an aging Pontiac Grand Prix. Hank hurried to get the door for me and he grabbed the handle and pulled. Off it came.

"Now that's never happened before," he said with a puzzled look. "Sorry about that. Never mind, I'll just open it from the inside."

He rushed around and got in on the driver's side and opened my door from the inside. As I got in, he tossed the door handle over his shoulder to the back seat, where it landed with a clank on a pile with the other parts of the car that would no longer stay put. I pulled the door hard and, as it shut, the trunk flew open, the horn honked, and the interior light flashed on an off.

"Now that's never happened before," he said.

He twisted the key four or five times, and then a couple more, until the Grand Prix made a few wimpy coughs and finally turned over with a horrible roar and a shudder. He stepped on the gas and the car lurched forward, snapping my head back.

"Sorry about that," Hank said.

As we began our drive, I took a casual moment to look around inside. The dash was missing most of the usual knobs. In their place were various other items (pen tops, paper clips, wads of paper where there were once air vents) and a dozen sticky notes with detailed instructions on selected but important functions of the car. Take this entry, for example: *Air conditioner—Bang dash hard with fist, once; pull red paper clip to right half way, back left one quarter; bang dash with fist hard again.* Or this one (which left me more than a little nervous): *Brakes— Pump three times, shift into neutral, pump again until the right rear wheel burns rubber, yank into low gear, back into neutral, and then push down on brake pedal until your foot cramps.*

"I know what you're thinking." Hank looked defensive as I eyed his use of ordinary office supplies. "I assure you, these are not our company's supplies!" With that, he twisted the steering wheel left and right, and each time he did this the wheel sent out a grating squeal, not unlike the sound of a creaking door in a haunted house, only much louder.

We were now roaring down the street at about 60 miles per hour. I pointed to the speedometer and suggested to Hank that he might be going too fast. He looked at the dash and just gave me a wide grin. "You know, I think the odometer is working again," he said. "Oh, hey, and the speedometer, too." He stepping on the gas and watched the needle climb. The steering wheel squealed again. The muffler's rumble hurt my ears.

Just then we came upon a man obviously struggling to change his tire on the shoulder of the roadway. Hank's face turned serious, determined, and he immediately did everything his sticky note said to do to stop the car. We came to a full stop two inches behind the man's car, but well ahead of the cloud of burning rubber behind us. In less than a minute, Hank was out of the car, had changed the man's tire, and was back in the Grand Prix, screaming down the road again.

A moment later he got a funny look on his face. At the next intersection, he burned more rubber making a hard right turn. A mile or two down the road, well into a wooded area, Hank suddenly came to a complete stop and jumped out of the car and, within two minutes, got a cat down from a tree, freed a raccoon from a hunter's trap, and escorted two deer and a family of armadillos across the road.

Back in the car, 60 miles per hour again, burning rubber, more terrifying car noises, that funny look on Hank's face.... Over the next three hours, and over most of St. Tammany Parish, I was a witness as Hank walked six ladies across the street, pulled a child from a burning building, found homes for a box-load of stray kittens, halted a convenience-store robbery (which was concluded, incidentally, when he convinced the robber to give back the money and free the hostages), changed five more flat tires, counseled three couples with troubled marriages, jump-started an 18-wheeler, and transported sixteen hitchhikers to various distant destinations.

Although I had done nothing during the entire journey, I was exhausted by the time we pulled up at my house. As for Hank, all he could say was: "See, I told you. It's exactly ninety-five miles to your house." ∎

# The French Quarter

The French Quarter. It wasn't the best of times; it wasn't the worst of times. It was June, and it was hot, as it always is in New Orleans in the summer, and my live-in girlfriend, Christine, and I were down in the French Quarter for a day of jazz and drink and shopping for T-shirts. If you ever need a T-shirt, you just have to come to the French Quarter. Forget about art, Cajun music, historic architecture—the T-shirt is what it's come to, but we've got the best.

We had just walked out of a shop on Bourbon Street when I spotted a small crowd down Conti, near Royal; Christine and I hurried over to see what was up. It was a transvestite conked out on the sidewalk outside a greasy bar.

One of the onlookers, a tourist from Iowa wearing Bermuda shorts he'd taken out of mothballs just for this trip, seemed the most concerned. "Do you think she's dead?" he asked me as I shoved my way through.

I looked at him, and then again, making sure he knew I was doing a double take, and said: "That's not a woman. That's a man."

He didn't believe me. "If you look real close," I said, "you'll see a five o'clock shadow under that makeup." So he bends down, looks real hard, and then comes back up scratching the bald part of his head. "Now I've seen everything," he said.

"How long have you been in the Quarter?"

"Oh, about a day."

"Then you haven't seen anything yet."

I left him in a stupefied state and called the police from the corner T-shirt shop. When I got back, the transvestite was sitting up, moaning. The bald tourist from Iowa just stood there and stared at him, like he'd never seen a man in a dress before. Christine and I headed up Royal Street for more T-shirt shopping.

About an hour later, we were at Jackson Square. It was crowded with tourists and other T-shirt shoppers and clumps of street entertainers—jazz, tap dancing, mime, acrobatics—and a guy playing music on the rims of little glasses of water. For just a minute or two I stopped and watched a redhead with long legs and a short skirt, but in that brief time Christine disappeared. I thought I caught a glimpse of her walking down Saint Ann, and hurried after her, but she vanished. This was exasperating me, and it was hot, and I wanted a drink of something cool.

I slipped into a nearby bar. It was dark inside. As my eyes adjusted to the light, I hopped onto a bar stool and asked the bartender for a Coke. He looked at me like I didn't belong there, but I was too thirsty to care. I paid him for the soft drink and took two long drinks. Suddenly I sensed someone directly behind me. There was a moment of heavy breathing.

"Hey, guy," said the smooth, distinctively male voice behind me, "would you like me to push that stool in for you?"

WRONG BAR! I took a quick drink of my Coke, partly to appear casual and un-nervous, partly as an emergency measure against my thirst, and partly to give me a moment to distract this fellow's attention while I dashed for the door. I used the old "Say, isn't that Bette Midler over there!" and I was gone.

Outside it was hot. Solar flames forced sweat from every pore of my body. I staggered down Saint Ann. After a few weak steps, a voice whispered to me. I turned to face a snub-nose revolver in the hand of a masked robber in a narrow alley. He took my wallet and was disappointed with what he found. I explained that I was a writer and kept my millions in Swiss francs and only my agent had the key to the vault and she didn't always return my calls. That just pissed him off more. He had me take my clothes off and then left me in my shoes and boxers in the alley. At least I was cooler.

I slinked down the alley. Coming upon a wooden fence, I looked over and spotted a clothesline with fresh wash hanging out to dry. I found the latch to the gate and did a dash to the clothesline. The only thing dry enough to wear was a flower-print dress. I threw it on. It was a perfect fit, except for all the areas where I differed greatly from the big-boned woman who owned the dress. I fled out the gate and down the alley.

The dress was cool, but it didn't stop the heat. I needed water. I was feeling faint. I rested against a house a minute or two and then started down the alley again. I saw movements of people in the distance. Reaching the end of the alley, I peered around the corner and spied Christine at a street-side clarinet concert. Safe at last! She could drive the car around and pick me up and take me home for water and pants. I called out to her, but she didn't hear me. I started toward her, and promptly passed out on the sidewalk.

When I came to, Christine was bending over me, waving a cheap Japanese folding fan in front of my face. Next to her was the bald tourist from Iowa.

"Help me," I cried out weakly.

"Here's two bucks, fella," said the tourist, taking a couple of bills from his Bermuda shorts and shoving them down the front of my dress. "You just gotta go buy yourself some new make-up." ∎

# Where a Man Plays There Will His Heart Be Also

---

Between Tuesday and Thursday, the day I was to go to Ellen Joulissaint's house to look over Robert's computer system, I was occupied with work, intermingled with trying again to straighten up my office. I had three networking jobs to take up my time. The first was to string together twelve PCs into a working connection of computing power for an insurance firm. The second was to tie three older PC systems into a new large server with a multi-gigabyte hard drive for a furniture store. And the third, which was taking more time than it deserved, required that I wander around a busy surgical practice and somehow plug four totally different kinds of computer system into a new one—and then stretch this across two parishes by way of broadband access, to connect this practice with two other satellite offices.

Was I happy? In a sense, yes, I was happy. But only because I was working for myself. I didn't have a job, nor did I have a career: I was a lone wolf eye-of-the-tiger metaphor-mixing maverick guy who was working for no one but myself. I also wasn't making the kind of money I made as a hospital administrator, but I hated that job. More specifically, I hated having to get up in the morning in accordance with someone else's agenda and having to work according to someone else's schedule and getting home knowing that I'd have to do the same thing all over again tomorrow, because I worked for someone else, which is what a job is all about. In my new situation, I set my own hours (within reason, of course) and have no one to answer to but myself. Admittedly, the hours are long but the rewards are many, the chief one being that I get to see the fruits of my labors as my own. The downside to all of this do-what-you-love-the-money-will-follow, however, is that I have to work doubly as hard to get the same dollars I got when I worked for someone else. The reason—which is not always the same for all other entrepreneurial businesses—is that I alone have to be drone, schlepper, marketing strategist, bookkeeper and file clerk, gofer, accounts receivable, accounts payable, collections department, go-make-coffee secretary, receptionist, salesperson, and also chairman of the board of directors, composed of me and a mirror.

I wouldn't have it any other way. So I tackled each of my tasks with the same energy equally, and with more enthusiasm than if I were working for someone else.

At some point in time, Thursday arrived. I drove over to Ellen's house, in a subdivision about two miles from ours. It was a smallish, Cajun-style cottage, like a hundred others in the area. They are popular with the changing population on the north shore of Lake Pontchartrain. This is a population that demands to look like everybody else. The Cajun-style cottage is a two-story house, but not really two stories. The second story is really the attic, outfitted for living and sleeping. They are pretty houses and give a functionality that could only have been inspired by life in Louisiana. We have no basements here, because a foot below the mud is water; so, when your foundation is on a mud bottom, the only place left to go is up—and that's exactly what a Cajun-style cottage does. As a small house with a big attic, the house is increased in living size by setting up the attic for living quarters. The overall impression of size is embellished by the use of double dormer windows, which also effectively completes the attic's disguise as a second story, and by raising the house up, either on a slap or on pilings. You are of course left with a house without an attic and without a basement, which is why it's called a cottage, I suppose. They used to be affordable, and considering their size you would think that they would remain a low-priced home, but the demand for them is so great that their price has risen appreciably and remains high.

Like most such cottages, Ellen's house had a tin roof laid out in sheets that overlapped in long rectangular sections. The sheeted tin roof is shinier and during rainfall noisier than the corrugated tin roofs to be found on some cottages, but it is more attractive, and in the case of the Joulissaint house it was a nice complement to the slate-colored wood siding that covered the exterior.

I pulled into the driveway. A two-car garage, with a tin roof that matched the house, stood ahead of me at the end of the drive, situated at a short distance beyond the house. I parked beside the house. I pulled my black tool bag from the back seat of the car and started up the brick walkway to the front porch, where Ellen was waiting for me.

Ellen Joulissaint is a slim, attractive blond, a little under 5-and-a-half feet tall, coming to about the middle of my chest. She keeps her hair cut shoulder length, with bangs that hang an inch from aqua eyes that had a hard time looking at the same thing for more than a few seconds. She has a sense humor, but you have to hunt for it and are never sure if what you think is funny will get one of her short, husky laughs, out of a small mouth that never opens wide, or whether you will get just a quizzical glance.

"Hi, Ellen," I said on my way up the walk.

"I heard your car," she said as I started up the steps. "Thanks for coming."

"Hey, it's a pleasure," I answered. Once I reached the porch, Ellen gave me a searching look, but with such disciplined determination that I almost stepped backward. The look was one of both pain and longing, perhaps an attempt to discover whether I was really friend or foe, whether I would hurt her by something I would say or bring her a little joy by helping her recall some event from her past with Robert. My response to her serious gaze was a smile, and after that she invited me inside.

"How is the new house?" she asked. "Are you enjoying it over here?"

"Ah, we love it." I followed her into the house. "We're just about settled in. Kim and Marshall have their own rooms, finally. Marshall is happy in his new school and Kim, well, she's had to make some adjustments in the change of schools, and to high school, and to an all-girls' Catholic school, but she's resilient."

"Robert loved his computer," she said matter-of-factly, leading me down the hall toward the study. "He would sit for hours in front of that thing. Especially late at night. He had games—which he really didn't play—and some programs with pictures and sounds—with multimedia—isn't that what it's called? Anyway, his biggest thing was his modem and dialing up bulletin boards around the country. He ended up spending most of his time on the Internet, but I think he liked bulletin boards more. He had a couple of special interest groups—those are called SIGs, you know—that he liked to join in on, things such as cats, model airplanes, and books, I think. Here's his desk. He spent a lot of time here. Too much, I think."

All the while she spoke she kept looking around, very subtly, as though she expected someone to appear. Still, she was telling me things I knew already; perhaps she knew that, but then a lot had happened to make her forget.

I looked at the desk. I was familiar with his system. He and I would chat about it and tinker with it during social visits: the last one was a barbeque about three months ago. Refreshing my memory, I started a mental inventory of the hardware he had on the desk, following cables that snaked outward to various other boxes, some familiar, some not, beside the system itself, on the floor, and above it on shelves. Anyone could tell right away that Robert loved telecommunications. He had two unplugged older modems sitting on the shelf above his unit; next to them was an external high-speed modem with trailing connections to his tower unit sitting below the desk, on the right. His main Internet connection was provided by a separate line which stretched from its wall jack to a DSL modem and finally to a port behind the system. His monitor was a 22-inch color screen. Very little else was evident about his system without pulling it apart and inspecting the insides. I knew that it was a fast Pentium, but the whole thing was an off-brand, available at some local computer shops or at a big discount through mail-order. Robert's interest in multimedia, the mix of sight and sounds in applications and documents, just about required that he have a sound board and a video accelerator inside the box. Two large book-shelf speakers with connections to the back of the system said immediately that his computer was equipped for stereo sound. Headphones, still teth-ered to the computer, were perched on a shelf above.

I did another quick inspection. One good indicator of an intelligent man's interests (if not an insight into his character) is what he reads. On the shelf above his system was a small bookshelf of basic computer reference books, including some manuals on sound and graphics. From that I in-ferred that one should expect to see much of that sort of software, along with the hardware that it needed, inside the box on his desk.

"Now, what exactly do you want me to do?" I asked Ellen. "Do you want to sell it? Do you want it organized for your children's use—perhaps you want to use it yourself?"

"Well, yes."

"Yes—which?"

"I'm not sure. I really don't know anything about computers. I'd like you to tell me what I should do with all this."

"First of all, let me ask you this: Is it too painful to have around? The equipment, I mean."

"No ... not really."

"Would you use it if you kept it?"

"I could learn how, couldn't I?"

"Yes, you could."

"And the children could use it for school. They have a computer lab now, and they'll need to know how to use it. Okay, you've convinced me—we'll keep it."

"That's a wise choice. Selling it, well, you never get back what you paid for it. That's just the way it is with this technology. In many ways it's like cars. Now, if you'll give me a few minutes, I'll just hack around here and see what Robert added since the last time he and I fooled around with this. It shouldn't take me long. I'll just do some minor re-organizing, if necessary, so it's easier for you to use what's here."

"Oh," Ellen said. "Sure, go ahead. Would you like some coffee, or a soft drink? I'm forgetting my manners."

"No, I'm fine," I said, sitting in Robert's desk chair and pulling the keyboard toward me.

"I'll be puttering around. Holler if you need anything."

"Great," I answered. I reached for the control panel's master switch and flipped it and all the lights on the console lit up and the computer gave forth a soft whir as it started its booting process. The monitor flickered on and the hard drive completed its chirping as the final boot process finished.

The desktop came up. With mouse and keyboard I went to work making an inventory of what Robert had stored here, what might be used by a widow and her three children, what reorganization I might be able to do on Robert's behalf, in his absence. As I did this, Ellen returned and stood directly behind me. Sipping a cup of coffee, she watched everything I did.

"I hope you don't mind," she said after a loud sip of coffee.

"No, that's all right. I'm just rooting around here, trying to find out what Robert's got that might be useful for you all. Computing is fun, but it can be productive, too, but only if you know where everything is and what you've got to work with. He's added a lot of stuff; some of it I've never seen before."

"I can tell you," said Ellen, "that's where our time together went. He used to tell me how he'd get just loads and loads of free stuff over the Internet, the Web—in addition to all the chatting he'd do. He'd just clack and clack away at that keyboard. Other times, he'd mouse around with some new graphics program or put his headphones on and enjoy some new music program."

"That was polite of him."

"What was?"

"Using headphones with a music program. I would've plugged in twenty inch speakers and let 'em rip. I know—I've done it. Used to drive Christine crazy with deep bass, rhythm, European and techno-pop tunes."

"I'm pretty sure he's got all that on this system. Marc, do you think Billy might find a use for it with his music interests? He's taking piano lessons and this just might keep his interest going. What do you think?"

"I think that's a great idea. If Robert does not, I've got a great music tutorial program. I've never used it, but it's gotten rave reviews. We'll need to add a MIDI interface and a keyboard—"

"—Now, don't let me interrupt you," she said, interrupting me. "You just keep doing what you're doing and let me know what you think. I'll just be around the house here. Let me know if you need anything." With that she wandered back to the kitchen, leaving me to putter around with Robert's system.

Hey, what's this? It was a folder full of graphics and sound programs and files. I didn't spot it before because it was just labeled with "XX." After a second, it was obvious what was in the folder and why it was labeled as it was. It was full of GIFs, JPEGs, PNGs, AVIs, MPEGs, and binary files, some very large, with titles such as: FIST, GIRL, TOPLESS, WITHCOW1, COLLEGE18, ANA07, GAGGEDX2, JANINE15, MADONA1, LITTLETEEN, PET4, SARANWRAP, TIEDBIKE, PIERCED03, BIZARRE69, CATFURRY. The thumbnail images revealed plenty. Being a man in his prime, and with a detached scientific interest, of course, I browsed through a few of the files.

No man will ever openly admit this, but somewhere well-hidden in his house is something that he considers especially erotic. Now, whether this was Robert's hidden cache or not, I don't know, but it was definitely a collection of pornographic pictures and video. The larger multimedia files were in their own subdirectory folder. There were about ten of them, all very large, and each with a frank title suggestive of what was contained in the file. One of these, *Mediterranean Delicacies*, seemed tame enough in title. It was also a recent addition to his collection, judging by the date of installation. It was a self-running program that did not require any utility for image-viewing. Since it contained sound, I pulled Robert's headphones from the shelf above and held one to my ear as I clicked the program to start.

"Mediterranean delicacies," said a woman's soft sultry voice as scenes of European fruits began appearing on the screen. The fruits were nice. I mean just the basic fruit groups from Europe, neatly arranged in the traditional wooden bowl, each with a cluster of grapes spilling over the side. The first bowl contained dates, figs, oranges, and apples; other bowls contained fruit of the less than decorative variety, such as potatoes, rice, sugar beets, olives, sprigs of wheat and rye, corn, peas, two giant mottled tobacco leaves, a wide array of nuts, and some fruit-stuffs I had never seen before. Behind each bowl, setting the scene for this festival of natural foods, were different scenes of Mediterranean cities and resorts: The Spanish Barcelona, Majorca and Valencia; Monte Carlo; Marseilles, Nice, St. Tropez and the Riviera in France; the island of Malta; Naples, Rome, and Venice; Palermo on Sicily; Algiers, Tripoli, Tobruk, Tunis, and Alexandria on the North African coast; Tel-Aviv; the island of Rhodes; the ruins at Knossos on Crete and at Mycenae and Athens. But I'm not a geography whiz and I know these places only because each picture named the place in a box centered at the bottom of the screen. And all of this was straightforwardly boring—until the girls came on.

Suddenly there was a beach scene with twenty girls standing together in a group, representing every natural hair color, each one wearing a bikini as skimpy as could be without being considered nude. They were then each introduced by name and vital statistics, and then the hard drive started whirring and the introduction began again, this time with video. The first girl—an alluring, smiling blond named Babbette—began removing her bikini, little piece by little piece, and moved rhythmically in an erotic posturing; then with slow and careful movements of her legs she began showing me every part of her naked female body.

A small creak of hallway wood shook me. I heard the small patter of Ellen's footsteps. In a panic I reached over to the power console and flipped the main switch, shutting down the entire system. The headphones flew out of my hand.

Hot coffee in hand, sipping loudly from the cup, Ellen walked up and stood close, behind me. My hands were shaking. I twisted quickly in the chair. I caught the smell of her perfume, a delicate odor of flowers and musk—

"—Did I startle you?" she asked. She smiled. She was holding her coffee cup with both hands.

"Yes ... you did," I stammered. "I was just testing the endurance of the hardware here."

"Is there anything I should see?"

"No, really, I don't think so," I said.

"Are you all right, Marc? You looked flushed."

"Oh, I'm fine—believe me. I shouldn't be much longer."

"Take your time," she said. "It's nice to have a man around the house again." With that she walked back to the kitchen, with a delicate sway to her hips.

I powered up the system again. I then spent the next few minutes on some simple reorganization, intent on making the system useful for Ellen and family, and especially eager to hide Robert's cache of eroticism from those whom it was not intended. I threw them all into a new directory and used my encryption software to shield this from anyone's eyes but my own.

72

I shut the system down again and went into the kitchen. Ellen was sitting at the kitchen table with a folder before her and papers in piles and strewn loosely in front of her.

"I'm finished with the computer," I said. "I did a little reorganization, but for the most part it's a well-put-together system, with lots of software for you and the kids to use. If you'd like, I'll come back and spend some time with you all, showing you what's what and how to get started. As for using the software, well, you can just jump right in, or maybe enroll in a course at the community college—"

"—That's a good idea," she said with a distracted look. "Can I call you?"

"You can call me any time—you know that."

"There's a void inside me, you know, and I need it filled, and I'm not sure how to do it." Her eyes bespoke a deep sadness and longing, and I became increasingly uncomfortable as she continued to stare up at me. "But I have these papers and lots of other things to get out of the way. Robert's death left a lot to do. But I'll get it done."

"I know you will," I said. "I'm going to let myself out. Call me when you want me to come back."

"Okay." She smiled wanly. "Thanks again, Marc." Her voice was sultry, and sad in a beckoning way.

I left her at the kitchen table. I picked up my bag by Robert's desk and walked out to the car. I sat with my hands on the steering wheel for a minute or two, and then took a deep breath and drove home. ■

# Louisiana Cat

After twenty years of marriage my wife decided to go to work full-time. I didn't make enough money for our lifestyle in our gated community, so she would leave the house through the front door in the morning and return the same way in the evening.

At her new job she met a woman who was moving with her second husband to Baton Rouge for their new life there, but they couldn't take their cat Gus and they wanted to know if we would take him. He was a large cat, she said, but a really loving, fun cat. He was at the vet's office, waiting; if no one would take him, she said, he'd have to go to the Humane Society and we all know what happens there.

So I went to the vet's to see Gus and he was the biggest American short-hair cat I'd ever seen. He was friendly, almost totally orange, but a little shy and stayed toward the back of what was really a dog cage until the friend, Beverly, reached in and took Gus out.

He was a handsome cat with inquisitive hazel eyes and enormous paws; he was neutered as a kitten and his front claws had been removed then, too. He wasn't sure what to make of me at first, and that was because he didn't get along with Beverly's new husband. Gus hated him, she said, and the new husband hated Gus. Once he left his briefcase open in the morning and before he left for work Gus jumped in it and peed all over his papers. That's why Gus wasn't going with them to Baton Rouge. He loved to stay on their screened porch and sit on a chair and look out, and whenever he wanted to play, he'd grab a toy in his mouth and walk on two legs towards you. There was a spark of intelligence in those cat eyes and he had personality, and I said we'd be happy to take care of Gus and we took the big orange cat home with us.

When he first got to the house, he stayed out of sight for about two days straight. I'm still not sure where he was—he was, after all, a really big cat—but he'd sneak out for food two or three times and to use the litter box. After that, he pretty much made himself very visible.

My children all loved him, although they couldn't handle his one big habit—in fact, I think I was probably the only one who could. If he liked you, he would get on the nearest countertop and jump onto your shoulders and stretch himself around your neck. He weighed about twenty-five pounds, so he was a lot to carry around, and he would stay like that until you pushed him off. The kids couldn't do that for more than a minute or so. He didn't give any warning that he was going to do the jump, so a few people were almost knocked over by this. I didn't mind it and could carry the weight, so Gus spent a lot of time on my shoulders.

He made friends with the family very quickly and once in a while he would come around the corner with a toy in his mouth, walking on his hind legs. He wouldn't walk too far like that, but perhaps he did it as often as he did because we always made a big deal about it, cheering and clapping to see this happy sight, and more so because as big as he was, he looked just like a toddler making his first steps.

We wouldn't let Gus outside. He had not been with us long enough and he wasn't at all an outside cat, so we had to stay vigilant about keeping him in the house. That was hard to do, with four children and their friends coming in and out of the house, but we were able to manage it for about four months. We didn't have a screened porch, so Gus struggled to find a way to look out on the world. I had a series of three tall windows in my study, so he made himself at home on the library table there and watched the world in the back yard from his new perch, until he made up his mind that he needed to see parts of the world that weren't visible from the table in my study.

One day we noticed that we hadn't seen Gus for several hours. We looked throughout the house for him and concluded that he had slipped out of the house.

Two days later a friend called me to say that there were remains of a large orange cat by the highway outside our subdivision. I made the children stay behind as I took a walk in that direction; I found him in the grass near the entrance to the neighborhood. He had been dead for at least a day; he was hit by a car, probably. I walked back to the house and then drove the car around with a shovel and a plastic bag. He was rotten and stinking in the hot Louisiana sun and the trunk of the car smelled like dead flesh for a week. I buried him in an out-of-the-way spot in the woods behind the house.

A year later my wife said she wanted a divorce and I knew then that Gus had loved me much more than my spouse. ∎

# Love in a Flash

---

Abby and I were in love for six months. That was as long as it lasted, short but hot, like the flame of gunpowder. We made love on the floor in my apartment in front of the 13-inch television where we had been watching a video of the movie *Phenomenon*. The floor wasn't my first choice, but the bed was only a single and I had no sofa. After my divorce, all I had was a rented apartment in Covington, Louisiana, the television, the single bed, a dining table, three computers, a stereo system, and a brown 1976 2-door Buick LeSabre with chipped paint and a bad transmission. Abby loved me in spite of it all.

She was tall, a natural blonde, a fitness trainer who could have been a model. She was also a Christian and I think we both struggled over the sex part, but I think, too, we planned to be together for a long time and making love seemed so very natural for us. We did that often, even if the floor was uncomfortable. She finally bought me a futon. Occasionally she spent the night, but she always left early in the morning before I got up.

In addition to the love making, which was good, we talked a lot. That was good, too. Abby was the only woman I remember ever talking so openly with, or felt free to talk openly with. Our first telephone conversations went on for about three hours each night. It was like high school again and I was in love for the first time. I was then 46 and she was 30 and still we could talk for hours every night. She lived in Hammond, about twenty-five miles away, and we didn't realize the cost of the toll calls until the end of the first month—and so then we just spent more time together.

We also wrote letters to each other. Mostly email, because that took less time and there's a pleasant immediacy to email. It also enabled us to type, so we didn't have to struggle with the tedium of the handwritten note. I was elegant and prolific and wrote some of my best love letters. They were poetic and lyrical and sweet and all the things that make love letters clever. She would write me back little darling pieces, always signing them with just the lower-case letter "a" and a period.

She had never married. From grade school through high school she was in a girls' boarding school and always felt, as a result, that something was missing from her emotional development. Her parents were divorced and she was reminded of the pain of that event whenever my children came over. She saw in their faces an emotion that I could not see. She told me this one night and cried. Eventually that pain became for her unbearable and she said that we couldn't see each other anymore. She took a job out of state and I never saw her again.

She sent me a Christmas card at the end of the year. It arrived with postage due. ■

# L'Improbable

On Wednesday, a week ago, my friend Gavin tried to kill himself. He's a nice guy with a keen intellect and good sense of the creative, and it was his excellent use of these attributes that led him to the clever suicide method he chose. He wanted the deed to be clean and efficient. Everything in its place, like his apartment.

He did his research. The gun was too messy: you couldn't be sure that a shot to the head would yield immediate death, and he wasn't keen on the gun-barrel-in-the-mouth technique, although that's usually a sure thing. He thought about the shotgun, but he imagined the horror at the splatter on the walls of his living room. He considered using the shotgun outside, but he wanted to be sure that his body would be found, and he wasn't comfortable with the thought that his body would end up lying in the sun for several days, the bloating feed bag of scavengers. Similarly, he discounted throwing himself under a train or in front of a fast car or truck.

Poison was out. You had to ingest it (drink it, chew it, swallow it) and that meant contending with the metabolic system and he wasn't much of a chemist, anyway, and that itself ruled out the injection. He wanted this to be a sure thing. Well, there was gas, but his accommodations were all electric, so that didn't make his list either. He didn't favor electrocution, so he moved on to other ideas.

He thought hard about using carbon monoxide and he could use his car and a hose for that, but he decided against it because he wasn't sure that it would be foolproof and he had a fear of waking up in the hospital still alive but brain damaged. He also didn't like the smell of car exhaust.

And then there was the knife and the many ways he could cut himself to get a good arterial bleed. It had to be a good bleed, because we have the clotting factor and the blood flow has to be sufficient to get past that. The wrist slash would hurt too much; he wasn't sure that his aim would be good enough for him to cut his own carotid artery, even with the aid of a mirror, and he couldn't picture himself fumbling with a sharp knife trying to do something as important as killing oneself. Plunging a knife or ice pick into the heart might work, but he really had a problem with the pain part, so that too was scratched off his list.

The bridge suicide was also ruled out. Gavin lived in a village in rural New York. There aren't any really tall bridges in rural upstate New York and he thought he might talk himself out of it if he took a plane to San Francisco. There were the gorges in Ithaca and high bridges in the Hudson Valley, but for this deed he wanted to be sure that it would be a success, that he would actually die and not end up with fractures and brain damage at the bottom of a long drop. There was, of course, the Empire State Building, or any of the other really tall structures in the big cities, but he hated the thought of the mess he would make on the sidewalk below, and he couldn't be sure that he wouldn't land on a person walking below. He wanted this to be a suicide, not manslaughter. Drowning was scratched from his list because he disliked the pain of not breathing. For several reasons, then, Niagara Falls was out.

He thought hanging might work for him—after all, many famous criminals were dispatched using that death method. As it happened, he had an aesthetic objection to that method, effective though it might be.

As he was cutting lettuce for his salad one evening about two months ago, he thought of the ideal method: Guillotine. Actually his first thought was the axe, and as he calculated in his head how he might axe himself to death, he hit upon the guillotine. It was clean and quick and ensured death. It was painless, or at least he thought that it would be painful for no more than a moment or so, and he could do the deed in his apartment, without much residual mess. Perfect. The guillotine is basically an angled knife suspended and dropped onto the neck, severing the head completely. He thought: Wasn't Saint Paul beheaded? Perhaps there is something to this guillotine thing. France made it famous, but it was last used for execution there in 1977. Gavin believed that he could revive it as a suicide machine.

So he set about building the guillotine. Or rather he set about finding a kit for it. The Internet yielded up several. He bought a kit for $295 from a company in New Orleans. It came in a large box, about the size of a seven-foot-tall artificial Christmas tree. Out of the box, it came with a large frame made from a recycled window sash, a super-sharp blade fashioned out of surplus plowshare, a narrow bench without padding, lower lunette (a notched block for the neck), and a basket made in Guatemala (for the head). The rope, to release the blade, was Indian hemp. It took him a week to assemble it, tightening everything with surgical steel bolts. I only got to see the thing last weekend, after it was all over.

But here's what happened. He erected the guillotine and set about testing it. He figured that the closest thing to the thickness and density of the human neck was a pineapple. He bought three of these at the supermarket and tried out the device on the heavy fruit. The first one only cut a quarter of the way through. He tried that again and again, each with the same result. So he figured he needed a heavier blade. The height was almost seven feet, but with the blade installed the distance between knife and his neck was only three and a half feet, since the stand had the victim lying less than two feet from the floor. That was enough to chop lettuce, but it wouldn't be sufficient to cut a pineapple, or a human neck. He couldn't increase the height, giving the blade greater acceleration, so he decided to put weights on the blade's frame. He hammered in two large nails and hung up two 10-pound weights from his workout weight set. That did the trick. With those weights hanging on the blade frame, he successfully cut straight through the other two pineapples. That gave him confidence and he set about deciding on the date for his own execution—his suicide, that is. That would be Wednesday.

Everything was set up. He wore comfortable khakis and a collarless cotton shirt. He came to the event wearing socks with no shoes. In order to make sure that the guillotine wouldn't fail him, he hung up another set of 10-pound weights on the nails. He was showered and his hair was clean and combed. He laid a plastic sheet and bath towels all about the device and beneath the basket; he then stretched himself out on the narrow bench, placing his neck in the notched channel of the lower lunette, directly below the weighted blade.

He stared down into the basket made in Guatemala and pulled the hemp rope. Apparently he yanked too fast and that jarred the blade frame and the extra weights he had put up dropped off the nails and fell straight down on his head, knocking him out.

When Gavin was revived, he couldn't remember why he had set up this device and forgot all about the suicide. He pondered the device for a few days, and then pushed it off to the side and decided it would be good for slicing lettuce, cabbage, and pineapples. He still has a headache, but he can live with that. ■

# The Monger

New Orleans. It was one of the mixed blocks in the Garden District, the blocks that are no longer all white. I had just parked my car on a side street, off Prytania, and started the walk to St. Charles Avenue. It was a hot day, almost the end of May, and I stopped for a moment to tie my shoes. They were big shoes, black brogues, with wingtips so wide they could fly me over the sidewalks like Mercury on speed. From their depths sprouted two yellow striped socks made of a nylon polyester rayon mix that made my feet sweat. I bent down, laying my clipboard off to the side. I didn't have to tie my shoes, but it gave me a chance to appear casual, like I belonged in this neighborhood. I had to. The Monger would be watching.

I finished my shoe tying, grabbed my clipboard, and stood up again. I must have been bent over for about ten minutes, because when I got tall again and started to walk I got dizzy and did a quick dance backwards and then went down with a hard crack. No one came to my aid and I lay there on the sidewalk for another few minutes before getting up, this time slower. I started walking again. The time was three thirty.

I rounded Harmony Street and St. Charles and walked briskly past a tall three story renovated Victorian with a wrought iron cornstalk fence along the front that looked as out of place as a zipper on a car door. Two oak trees past the Victorian, I stood in front of a tidy pink shotgun house with green wooden shutters clinging to the sides of a tall split glass window that stood as tall as the front door to the right of it. The door could have been any door in the French Quarter. Green, like the shutters, with a polished brass doorknob sitting atop a lock that could be picked by any kid with a 30-piece tool kit from Sears. But this was Uptown. And this was the house of The Monger.

I opened the latch on the chain link gate and walked up the brick path and then up the short concrete steps to the porch, a lonely wide stretch of green painted wood. The instant my foot touched the porch, one of the slim boards left its mooring and slapped me in the face. I tottered back, lost my footing on the steps, and landed on my back on the

89

bricks. Struggling to my feet, dazed and sore, I checked my watch again. It was three forty five.

I picked my clipboard out of the grass, about ten feet away, and made my way back up the steps. The attack board had settled itself back into its hiding place on the porch. I stepped carefully, taking short steps, moving side to side, like a Brahmin in a cobra field, right up to the green door. The doorbell made a tinkling sound inside the house and I heard slow footsteps coming toward me. The door opened. A figure stood in the doorway. So this was The Monger.

"Good afternoon, sir." I gave him my biggest smile. I held the clipboard out in front of me. "How are you today?"

"What are you selling?" he asked. The Monger bought my act. He was shorter than I expected. His head was small, but shaped for thinking, and shiny bald, except for a few clumps of gray hair that clung to the sides, above two large ears. His etched brow was wide and his blue eyes set far apart on a narrow face. Beneath each eye was a hanging mass of wrinkles, suggesting sadness and guilt. A nose the size of an outfielder's throwing arm stared out at me. His mouth was small. The lips, so thin they could have been penciled on, twisted to the side and The Monger spoke again: "I haven't got all day. So what're you selling?"

"Well, sir, this is your lucky day. I'm not selling a thing. I'm with the ACME Research Company and we're in your area today conducting interviews for a survey commissioned by a consortium of clients seeking information on safety in the home and wherever people eat, sleep, shop and play." How I got all of that in one breath I will never know. But when you work undercover, you have to be prepared to make the act convincing. And I was a pro. I had to do it right. This man was no fool. He was The Monger.

"An interview? Hmm. I haven't been to an interview for thirty years. I used to be pretty good at it myself. My name's Johnny Cleaver." We shook hands through the doorway. "Hey, come on in," he said.

He backed away from the door and waved me in. The floors were wood, not parquetry but painted slats, like those on the front porch. I stepped inside cautiously, looking down, walking with wide slow steps, like a first lieutenant outside a Vietnamese hamlet.

"I got something for that jock itch," said Johnny Cleaver, a.k.a. The Monger, looking me up and down, over his shoulder.

"I'll be all right once I get to a chair," I answered.

"Have a seat here." He motioned me to a heavily padded black leatherette recliner in front of an oval black lacquered coffee table. On the other side of the table was a sofa, possibly a sofa bed, with a wide flower design printed on a heavy weave off-white fabric. He settled himself down into the center of the sofa and then stretched out, propping his head up on one of three big square pillows lounging near the arm rest. I sank into the recliner and propped my clipboard on my knee.

"Now, what exactly would you like to know?" he asked.

"Well, Mr. Cleaver, tell me." I looked down at my clipboard and pulled a pencil from the inside pocket of my herring bone jacket. I started scribbling nothing in particular on the top sheet of blank paper in my lap. "What is the first thing that comes to mind when you hear the word microwave oven?"

"A yuppie couple with the exploded remains of a dead kitten."

I knew it! This was indeed The Monger. But I just had to be sure. I had to get him to reveal himself to me. I said: "Are you familiar with the new Kitten Safe Microwave Oven, by Tao Kornung?"

"No—I'm not!" He sat up abruptly. Terror filled his wide eyes.

"Yes, it's the newest in a line of animal safe appliances designed to protect innocent people with money who haven't a clue as to how to operate today's modern machinery. Now, what's the first thing you think of when you hear the word carbonated beverages?"

"Why, um, syringes stuffed inside soda pop cans."

"Have you heard of the new Syringe Safe cans manufactured by Subway Aluminum for Popsie Cola Bottlers?"

"No. No, I haven't," said Johnny "The Monger" Cleaver who sat dejected on the edge of the sofa. I had him where I wanted him.

"Apples?" I asked.

"Razor blades."

"Halloween?"

"Apples with razor blades inside."

"Slides at water parks?"

"Razor blades," he said.

"I suppose, then, that you haven't heard that all razor blade manufacturers are planning to discontinue the distribution of single blade razors? And they expect to offer rewards and refunds on the return of all such blades sold in the past twenty years. Handsome rebates on the purchase of a new line of safety razors are also available."

"I don't believe it." He was standing now.

"Oh, but it's true."

"Impossible. You're just repeating a rumor. On the other hand, it can't be a rumor."

"And why not, may I ask?"

"Because I would know about it, that's why."

"Have you then heard that the dead body of Elvis has been positively identified?"

"Stop this! That's not true! I'd know about it if it were!"

"And just how is it you would know!" I was standing now. He glared at me. His hands trembled.

"Because, because—because I am THE MONGER!"

"AH HAH! So you admit it!"

"Yes, I admit it! Every major rumor in this country can be traced directly to me and my campaign to wake everyone up to the subtle dangers around them! I started small. Growing up in the fifties, I was the one who started the rumor about children locked in abandoned refrigerators. I alone was responsible for the spate of Hitler sightings and I also started the rumor about the truck driver who was driving along with his arm out the window—you remember, the one who had it severed by a passing vehicle and who drove for miles without realizing it. I almost gave up rumor mongering, when I turned to journalism. But I was no good at that and soon went back to mongering."

"Hey, how about snakes?" His thin lips became a smile. "Remember this one? A lady goes into the department store and tries on an imported fur jacket and feels pins sticking her in the back, only they're not pins but baby coral snakes, and she collapses and dies. Remember that? I'm proud of that one. How about the one about kids playing in the plastic balls in the hamburger restaurant's playground and getting bitten by water moccasins? That was mine, too. Oh, oh, but let's not forget my classic—"

"—Your classic?"

"Yeah, lest we forget. A baby alligator is flushed down the toilet and it grows up in the sewer system. That was mine. Really. They made a movie about it. And, oh, sure, I did the one about the yuppie couple who tried to dry out the little rain-drenched kitten in the microwave and ended up blowing it to bits. That was gross. I was having a bad day when I thought that one up. It was about the same time I invented the word *zit*. But I sure had some fun with all those Elvis sightings. I tell you, some people are just plain stupid. But my tour de force has got to be the one about the missing son."

"Refresh my memory."

"Well, this woman's son—he's about twenty or twenty-five—has been missing for over three days. It was not like him to be away that long without some word. She's worried and so checks with the police and they start looking for the young man, but discover nothing. Then, a few days later, he turns up as a John Doe in a major hospital. Turns out he had been mugged, robbed of his wallet and all identification, and left dead in an alley. The woman identifies her dead son at the hospital and the body is given over to a mortuary for burial preparations. At the wake—now get this—the mortician himself comes over to the grieving mother and offers his condolences and says, 'It's a terrible thing what happened to your son.' Of

95

course, she thinks he's talking about the fatal mugging. But then he says, 'I've never seen anything like it in my entire career.' And she asks him what he means, and he says that when he prepared the body he found that all of the man's organs had been removed."

"The hospitals didn't like that one," I said, pushing the hairs down on the back of my neck.

"Well, now you know," said The Monger. "What happens next? I suppose you're going to take me in?"

"I have to. It's my job."

"May I go to the bathroom first?"

I looked him up and down, and then nodded. I followed him to the opposite end of the living room and stepped in front of him as he lunged toward a tall door. I entered the bathroom. A flimsy flower print curtain obscured a small high window's light into the dark space. I flipped the light switch and took a cautious look around the small room. The tub was classic white, Queen Anne style, with those ridiculous feet; an ugly oval shower curtain hung in the middle. The toilet and wall hung sink were clean but stained. Strewn all around the floor were piles of yellow newspapers, faded tabloids, and dog-eared magazines.

"This is my reading room," he said, anticipating my question. "A man in my business has to stay on top of the latest news."

"I see that," I said. "Don't be long." I waved him into the bathroom and shut the door. I returned to the sofa and sat down, keeping my eyes on the bathroom door. Soon my eyes were watering; I looked at my watch. It was four thirty.

Just then I heard the grunt of a small man trying to lift a window that had not been opened since the last time it was painted, and then the unmistakable sound of a short man climbing through a bathroom window. I sprinted for the door! It was locked. I thrust my shoulder against it! The door did not budge. My shoulder hurt. I tried the other shoulder, and this time the door gave way and I fell face down into a pile of old *Reader's Digest* magazines. I looked up from the floor and watched as a breeze blew aside the torn curtain, revealing the open window. The time was four forty two. The Monger was gone.

I stayed in the house a few minutes longer to look for clues. I studied his phone records and read his mail, and then left. There was nothing more for me in the house. The Monger would not return.

I interrogated the neighbors. For days I watched his street. But he was gone from the city. I would never find him again.

From time to time, new rumors surface—some ridiculous, some ugly—and people are once again shaken and dismayed as companies are maligned, the safety of their products questioned in the press, and as the famous dead walk again among the living, and small fears are let loose to terrorize the uncritical masses.

97

As for me, I do what I can to quell the rumors as they appear, but I have found no one who will believe me when I tell them that one man alone is responsible for these desultory eruptions of fear. It is like trying to get a dog to lie down in the back of a moving pickup truck. But then, if I had come back from the end of the rainbow, I would expect people to ask me for a glimpse of gold, too. The Monger remains free, and he continues to elude me.

I put my pipe in the ashtray and take a long drink of whiskey and try to remember how Capablanca would calculate the relative value of Knight and Bishop. Suddenly I shudder and look at the drink in my glass and I think surely that I had read or heard that a few people had died after drinking this brand, and then I am not sure and I am overcome by a kind of doubt that would make The Monger smile. ■

www.ingramcontent.com/pod-product-compliance
Lightning Source LLC
Chambersburg PA
CBHW030528260626
47157CB00005B/1927